ear

Learn phonics with

Actiphons

Lear Disappear

Written by Teresa Heapy

Phonics consultant: Kate Ruttle

Physical literacy consultants: Dr. Lowri Cerys Edwards and Dr. Lucy Jane Griffiths

LADYBIRD BOOKS

UK | USA | Canada | Ireland | Australia
India | New Zealand | South Africa

Ladybird Books is part of the Penguin Random House group of companies whose addresses can be found at global.penguinrandomhouse.com.
www.penguin.co.uk www.puffin.co.uk www.ladybird.co.uk

Penguin Random House UK

First published 2021
001

Illustrations by Complete Control (UK) Limited

Printed in China

A CIP catalogue record for this book is available from the British Library

ISBN: 978-0-241-39067-2

All correspondence to:
Ladybird Books
Penguin Random House Children's
One Embassy Gardens, 8 Viaduct Gardens, London SW11 7BW

Tips for grown-ups

Name: Lear Disappear

Letter sound: **ear** as in 'disapp**ear**'

Favourite activity: mountaineering

Action: Squat down, then curl over your knees.

Actiphons is an energetic phonics programme designed for young learners.

Each of the 70 collectable stories stars its own playful character and practises their letter sound and action. By reading the stories in order, children will build their phonics skills and become active, lifelong readers.

How to help your child to read

- Read the words in small type and encourage your child to read the words in big type. Remind them to sound out and then blend together the sounds in each word to read it. For example, "**j-o-g**, jog", "**s-ai-l**, sail" or "**qu-i-ck-er**, quicker".
- If your child struggles with a word, help them to sound it out. If they still find it difficult, just read the word to them and move on.
- You can use the activities at the back of this book for extra practice. Have fun!

Lear Disappear loves to play hide and seek on the mountain.

She can crouch so low that she always wins!

Lear can wait in a good gap.

Lear is with her friends. Olly Obstacle counts to ten.

Swimming Sally, Physical Phil and Lear run and hide.

They all rush off. Lear is quick!

Phil finds a good place to hide.

He can wait near this rock.

The rock is very heavy, but Phil can lift it.

Sally heads for the lake.

The lake is a good place to hide.

It is hard to see Sally now.

Lear has hidden herself away, too.

Olly will never see her there!

She got into the gap with no fuss.

Olly comes to find them.

Huff, puff!
Huff, puff!

I can hear you, Phil!

Then Phil and Olly find Sally.

Everyone tries to find Lear.

Lear won the game!

ear

Your turn!

Can you crouch down low like Lear Disappear?

Squat down, then curl over your knees.

To see a video of this action, listen to the story or sing the song, go to **www.ladybirdeducation.co.uk**. Click **'Unlock book'** and enter this code:

cDaicYTUvf

What next?

Talk about it

- Who got wet during the game of hide and seek?
- How did Lear Disappear win the game?

Phonics fun

- Can your child find the **ear** sound in Lear's name? Emphasize the sound as you say the name.
- Give your child the book, and ask them to find and read three different words containing **ear** as quickly as they can.

Get active!

- Lear Disappear loves mountains! Ask your child to walk up and down a flight of stairs a few times, counting the number of steps they take. Then, ask them to walk on flat ground for the same number of steps. Which felt easier? Why do they think that is?

Turn the page to find your next Actiphons story!

Collect Actiphons Level 2